Acting Edition

New Golden Age

by Karen Hartman

No one shall make any changes in this title(s) for the purpose of production. No part of this book may be reproduced, stored in a retrieval system, scanned, uploaded, or transmitted in any form, by any means, now known or yet to be invented, including mechanical, electronic, digital, photocopying, recording, videotaping, or otherwise, without the prior written permission of the publisher. No one shall share this title(s), or any part of this title(s), through any social media or file hosting websites.

For all inquiries regarding motion picture, television, online/digital and other media rights, please contact Concord Theatricals Corp.

MUSIC AND THIRD-PARTY MATERIALS USE NOTE

Licensees are solely responsible for obtaining formal written permission from copyright owners to use copyrighted music and/or other copyrighted third-party materials (e.g. artworks, logos) in the performance of this play and are strongly cautioned to do so. If no such permission is obtained by the licensee, then the licensee must use only original music and materials that the licensee owns and controls. Licensees are solely responsible and liable for clearances of all third-party copyrighted materials, including without limitation music, and shall indemnify the copyright owners of the play(s) and their licensing agent, Concord Theatricals Corp., against any costs, expenses, losses and liabilities arising from the use of such copyrighted third-party materials by licensees. For music, please contact the appropriate music licensing authority in your territory for the rights to any incidental music.

IMPORTANT BILLING AND CREDIT REQUIREMENTS

If you have obtained performance rights to this title, please refer to your licensing agreement for important billing and credit requirements.

NEW GOLDEN AGE received its Off-Broadway premiere at Primary Stages (Andrew Leynse, Artistic Director; Shane D. Hudson, Executive Director; Casey Childs, Founder), May 2022. The performance was directed by Jade King Carroll, the scenic designer was Lee Savage, the costume designer was Jen Caprio, the sound designer was Fan Zhang, the wig, hair, and makeup design was by J. Jared Janas, the props designer was Carrie Mossman, the fight coordinator was Alex Might, the casting director was Stephanie Klapper, the production stage manager was Denise Cardarelli, and the assistant stage manager was Olivia Tymon. The play was presented as part of 59E59 Theaters' first annual AMPLIFY Festival (formerly VOLT) celebrating the work of Karen Hartman. The cast was as follows:

MAT . . . . Doug Harris
LIN . . . . Mahira Kakkar
POLLY . . . . Claire Siebers
SILAS . . . . Ricardy Fabre
JACE . . . . Carmen Castillo

NEW GOLDEN AGE was a Finalist for the 2023 International Susan Smith Blackburn Prize.

NEW GOLDEN AGE was supported by a Guggenheim Fellowship, SPACE on Ryder Farm, the Keen Company Writer's Group, and The Colorado New Play Festival.

SPECIAL THANKS

The author wishes to thank all the collaborators at Primary Stages and 59E59 Theaters, especially Val Day for envisioning the AMPLIFY Festival.

Also:

Workshop artists: Molly Camp, Erin Daley, Anastasia Davidson, Angel Desai, Susannah Flood, Jackson Gay, Chris Holtkamp, Lisa Hori-Garcia, Jen Jarnagin, David Alan Madrick, Deepa Purohit, ML Roberts, Emry Rockenield, Avery Trunko, Vincent Van der Velde, Noah Zachary.

The Keen Company Writer's Group: Lisa Ramirez, Jonathan Silverstein, Jeremy Stoller, Ken Urban. My longstanding New York writers group.

For time and generosity: Gordon Dahlquist, Eisa Davis, Lina Khan, Todd London, Anne Washburn, Chay Yew.

For getting this book into your hands: Skyler Gray, plus the team at Samuel French/Concord Theatricals especially Amy Rose Marsh, Garrett Anderson, and Ben Keiper.

CHARACTERS

MAT – A multibillionaire tech founder. First impression is warm, personable, and boyish. Mid thirties, male.

LIN – A professor and underground folk hero. Elegant and charismatic. Late forties, female.

POLLY – A gifted, unemployed performer. Lin's half-sister. Animated, emotional, and charming. Mid thirties, female.

SILAS – A rising star working for Mat. A superpower listener. Mid twenties, male.

JACE – The student leader of Lin's movement. Moral clarity where anger meets innocence. Also a singer. Early twenties, nonbinary (preferred) or female.

Lin looks East Asian or South Asian. Polly looks white. Mat looks white. Silas looks Black. Jace could be of any race.

SETTING

The world feels low tech and navigable. Consider practical lighting, or lighting with simple sources. No projections. We don't see phones, laptops, or other devices. Although this may seem seem like a play about technology, really it's about intimacy, so we want to feel close and real.

Lin's office is a high-status old-fashioned enclave in an Ivy League university. Dark wood. Crank windows. Homey touches like a plant or a candy bowl, but mostly this is a serious place full of paper. The door is important and wants a strong spot.

Elements of Mat's world (Sunlight) have been designed to evoke the ambient, tactile "past" of Lin's world.

TIME

One day in 2033.

AUTHOR'S NOTES

Lin's scholarly theories are partially derived from the writings of Lina Khan and Shoshana Zuboff. All other aspects of the play are fictitious.

Dialogue in (parentheses) is an unspoken thought.

Italics indicate a stressed word, and **bold** indicates bigger urgency.

Fear is a specific form of intelligence that comes when hindsight, insight, and foresight collide.
– Valeria Luiselli, "Things as They Are"

we are each other's
harvest:
we are each other's
business:
we are each other's magnitude and bond.
– Gwendolyn Brooks, "Paul Robeson"

New Golden Age is dedicated to Andrew Leynse (1969–2023),
in loving memory of his enthusiasm, generosity, and care.

PROLOGUE

Optional pre-show:

(**JACE** *enters. People are still settling.*)

(**JACE** *breathes.*)

JACE. Hey.

It's been a minute.

(*Breathes.*)

Would you please turn off your phones, anything that makes noise? I'll wait.

(*Breathes.*)

Look around. Get your bearings.

This is a play, but it's also a room.

(*Words in [brackets] can be omitted or varied.*)

[It has exits.]

(*Briefly describes the exits.*)

[Thank you for wearing your masks. Please keep them over your mouth and nose.]

(*Breathes.*)

We are here.

We are here.

(*Breathes.*)

JACE. We'll be here for about ninety minutes.

Or start here:

*(Darkness. **JACE** sings a cappella, ideally from somewhere else in the space.)*

OPEN YOUR EYE
PEEL BACK THE DAY
WELCOME THE LIGHT.
OPEN YOUR EYE
BEHIND THE LID
LIES GOLD
LET ME IN.
LET ME IN.

*(**MAT** talks earnestly to us. Natural vibe, gentle light. No headset or anything like that. **MAT** designed his world to feel warm and incandescent, like a memory of twentieth century film.)*

MAT. Hey hey from Sunlight! Good to connect, amiright?

Thanks for tuning in, with your Sunplants. We got three point nine...

(Taps a spot on his face or neck, to check.)

crossing into four billion of you gathered today. Right here:

(Taps the same spot.)

Sunplant to Sunplant. The best and safest way to connect.

I have a gift to reveal. I'm pumped! Sunlight Seedbank!

You ask: Mat, after all Sunlight has given us, why and how could you give us more?

I'll start with why.

We emerge from an experiment. A massive, involuntary, long term experiment. For some it was permanent, and we grieve.

(Pause.)

Pause Nine hurt. I missed you. I missed you in my gut.

But one morning, was it day forty-one, day three oh five, my twins traced each other on big paper, cut out "friends" to tape on the walls. My sons are my life. My sons and Camille, as your families are no doubt your lives.

Nine-year-olds made a society. What does that tell me?

We need to connect.

Now, I worked eighteen hours a day since I was twenty, aight, so I missed years with BB and Mazz. Camille stepped to that labor and that joy. But in this Pause, Papa Mat was home for bedtime!

It was a humbling experience. I recommend it. Bedtime! It takes forever! But in the end, so –

(Chef's kiss meaning "so close.")

This Pause helped a lot of us get to some new domestic levels, amiright?

I want that bond for you.

I want it for my boys.

Now: some forces want to block closeness. Some elites want to outlaw our bonds. They try to use grandma "schools" and arthritis "laws" against us. When you hear "Right to the Dark," ask yourself, what have human beings feared most for all of history? Were the Dark Ages awesome?

We are not going back.

MAT. And yet there's been – I admit it – a gap between what some like to call Real Life and the way we shared through first wave Sunlight: AwareHome, InLight learning, Sunplants.

Folks still seek that messy drippy bite, the friction and the rub.

It's 2033 but we want to feel analog. Cozy. We want to remember.

Which brings me to How.

Spoiler alert, the answer is not the Outer Plains! That would be sad, lonely, and dangerous!

It's so sweet. When you got your free Sunplants, communication chips right here...

        (Taps the same spot. It's an implant.)

that liberated you from clunky devices, *we* at Sunlight got a little sumpin sumpin that we didn't know how to use until now! We got your cells! Just a few, at the edge of the Sunplant.

And it turns out cells hold memories! *Wut wut!* Beautiful experiences, maybe tough experiences, even ancestors.

So what's the difference between the ways we already know you, and the new Seedbank Tale?

We are going to rebuild memory from your cells. Not eavesdropping, not eyeblink, the real you. Bio level.

Finally, we can share *you.*

Other people have always been our greatest source of pleasure and amusement. But other people bring plague and violence, amiright?

Seedbank Tales will transport you.

Make you feel that hug they call the Dark.

But safely, InLight.

We're even going to pay some of you.

Wut wut? Yasss!

If you are a Talent Worker who got lost in the Pause, now is your time.

We need you to help us shape the deep feels – sort these memories, weave the best of the Sunplant data, the squishiest stories, and make meaning.

Seedbank Tales.

Come do what you do again.

Bring on the truth. Pour out the clear raw juice.

This is culture! Get hype!

Together we will be so close.

Scene One

>(**SILAS** *and* **POLLY** *converse charmingly,
>holding mugs. He is beautifully dressed.
>She hasn't shopped in a while, but works
>what she's got. Flirty, high-wattage mutual
>fascination.*)

SILAS. But tell me about you. Who are you?

POLLY. Oh my god it's so kind that you care!

SILAS. That's what I do!

POLLY. If you're gonna know me, you should know about
my fam.

SILAS. Fam is all.

POLLY. I was married...to a great guy...who wanted terms
that did not work for me!

SILAS. Such as?

POLLY. I'm all: "Let's have a baby!" and Hubs was more:
"Let's group fuck a Walmart."

SILAS. Yeah that's pretty different.

POLLY. And muh name may be "Poly" but this girl is "Mono."

SILAS. *(Cracking up.)* So real.

POLLY. And I'm like...with what power can I step out of
this marriage and reset my terms? The power of TIME.

SILAS. YASSSS.

POLLY. Thus the egg freeze. TMI?

SILAS. I want all the I. All. The. I. No such thing as an
"ova-"share.

POLLY. *(Cracking up.)* Ova!

I did not expect this to be so –

SILAS. Click?

POLLY. Click, hells yeah even a –

SILAS. Boom?

POLLY. Boom.

SILAS. If I were female, I would freeze, definitely. Why be tied to bio?

POLLY. It's freedom.

SILAS. With adequate time, you can equalize any imbalance.

POLLY. Such as: if procreation is *natural* why is it *fuckin impossible* to raise kids without a gatrillion dollars?

SILAS. That right there.

POLLY. To have a job you need to *give* a job; you personally must personally pay for every hour you get paid. How is that math?

SILAS. It's not math.

POLLY. It's ass math.

SILAS. I mean there's AwareHome, for the gaps.

POLLY. A camera is not care!

SILAS. Respect.

POLLY. So as a Talent Worker, and as a lady, I chose to disrupt.

SILAS. I like it.

POLLY. Yay!

> (**SILAS** *offers* **POLLY** *an energy bar. She eats it weirdly fast.*)

SILAS. I can't be compelled by a victim. I won't identify because...

Self Preservation of the Mind. I could. I could get Woe is Me and focus on racial circumstances –

POLLY. *(Mouth full.)* And you would be *so justified* –

SILAS. You could go Woe is Me on the gender aspect. But we don't.

Which makes us heroes of our own lives. And that's attractive. You're attractive.

POLLY. Thank you.

SILAS. Put me in some kind of driver's seat or I'm out the car!

POLLY. I hear that.

SILAS. Find a way – always – that the victim is also the perp.

POLLY. And vice versa!

SILAS. So, you ditch multi-player man and reclaim your time!

POLLY. My mom paid for the procedure.

SILAS. GO MOM. Are you like –

(Chef's kiss meaning "so close?")

POLLY. Truth, my mom is quite basic and we don't connect? But when I regard her in context I feel compassion. Utter compassion.

SILAS. Like an empathy?

POLLY. I wish it were an empathy. Though this is where my mom –

(Super moved but keeps it together.)

My mom is a fuckin hero. She grew up end of the twentieth with all the toxic misogyny of that era, but turned it around in one generation, raised me *without* the self-loathing; so I don't empathize because I don't carry her same burdens, but that's because *she* unburdened *me*!

SILAS. My folks are immigrants so I feel you. They drag something I don't. They flourish through me.

POLLY. Tell me more!

SILAS. So, Mom is basic but a hero.

POLLY. And she wants romance.

SILAS. We need to connect.

POLLY. YAS. So she's beating the odds, fighting her own lady-clock… you know where I'm going –

SILAS. I do not.

POLLY. Surgery!

SILAS. *(Positive.)* Oh shit.

POLLY. Yeah, while I'm all –

> *(Mimes shots in her ass with a chakka chakka sound.)*

Mom's doing –

> *(Chakka chakka for botox, brow, and mouth.)*

SILAS. Oh you're wicked!

POLLY. Her face goes smooth and kind of –

> *(Makes a blank happy face.)*

And Mom's losing her hearing so her expression goes all Alert Barbie like –

> *(Alert Barbie face.)*

Which is charming, but –

SILAS. You lose your connection.

POLLY. *(YES YOU UNDERSTAND.)* I *lose* my connection to my *mom*.

SILAS. So deep.

POLLY. You want this?

SILAS. I want it all!

POLLY. Then when it's time for my egg harvest she late-books full face and neck, *in MexiCal.*

SILAS. Damn.

POLLY. She paid my med fees but now she wants me to cancel and be her person, like change her bandages, and I'm just –

SILAS. *(A little extra as Polly.)* **Fuck you, Mom!**

POLLY. Not those words, but –

> *(In conversation with Mom.)*

Mom, don't you want the future?

Instead of trying to smooth your way to the past?

(To **SILAS**.*)* Back in the day Mom could wreck you with an eyebrow. Her face was a superstore of emotion.

SILAS. And to shut off all those aisles...

POLLY. YAS, between the deafness and the Resting Alert Face my mom is literally becoming a wax replicant. Meanwhile my hormones amplify feels 'til I'm ugly crying "Yo I need you, yo don't do this, Mommy keep your faaaace –"

SILAS. Did you go to her surgery?

POLLY. No. I chose the eggs.

SILAS. Who went?

POLLY. My sister. Half, on my dad's side.

SILAS. Ah, so it wasn't her face.

POLLY. *(YES YOU UNDERSTAND.) It wasn't her face.* She goes in my place which I appreciate but also...

SILAS. Also?

POLLY. Full disclose do not appreciate?

SILAS. Why?

POLLY. My sister is uber-righteous.

SILAS. Yeah?

POLLY. So I like need but also do not need for her to assume my duties.

SILAS. So Lin goes.

(Weird that **SILAS** *said "Lin," but* **POLLY** *doesn't miss a beat.)*

POLLY. Lin goes.

SILAS. Win win!

POLLY. Sure!

SILAS. Go Mommy! Go Polly!

POLLY. Yay!

SILAS. How does she look?

POLLY. **She died!**

SILAS. What.

POLLY. She totally never woke up! Anesthesia error.

SILAS. Your mother *died*?

POLLY. Deadass.

SILAS. Of a facelift?

POLLY. That makes her sound shallow but yeah, of the prep.

SILAS. This was when?

POLLY. Three weeks?

(Beat.)

SILAS. Where do we go from here.

POLLY. We pivot! In this Seedbank Tale I see the circle of life – Mom dies of elective cosmetic shit while girl in her prime chases base functionality – three generations, all compromised, all for sale, yet the *choices* within that! We lean into the choice, Silas! We drive the fucking car!

(This was an interview and it's over.)

SILAS. Grand.

Jocelyn will walk you out.

(POLLY *stands, holding her coffee.)*

POLLY. I truly believe folks everywhere will respond, especially the way the Seedbank Tales will resurrect body memory. Mom never got a Sunplant but I kept her hairbrush so the cells are right there. We can reconstruct all the feels!

SILAS. Would you be willing to eat your mother's hair to get her memory cells?

POLLY. I'm in!

SILAS. *(Kind.)* For this phase it's too niche.

POLLY. Niche, I mean technically women are like half the people...

SILAS. I wish I were God.

POLLY. I can't pay.

SILAS. Oh this was free.

POLLY. They're gonna repurpose my eggs.

SILAS. Kay.

POLLY. Deposit expires tomorrow.

SILAS. Kay.

POLLY. Not Kay. Nokay.

SILAS. You have family.

POLLY. My mom left debt.

SILAS. You have Lin.

POLLY. I can't ask Lin. I need this gig.

SILAS. Fam is all.

(*Micro-beat.*)

POLLY. Silas, why am I here?

SILAS. You know your resources. Jocelyn?

POLLY. You called me in to get to Lin. Not my ideas. Not my Introvid.

SILAS. Your Introvid was fire, for real.

POLLY. I didn't get to fully convey, I am so pumped for Seedbank Tales. As a highly-trained talent worker with mad empathy skills, I will weave, spin, and crush whatever cell memories you choose into a bio-level share that goes deep. I am all about meaning.

SILAS. (*Cheerful, at no point sinister.*) We know what we need. You know what you got.

POLLY. I can't offer my sister.

SILAS. We love Lin.

POLLY. Don't bullshit me.

SILAS. She's grassroots and she's wise.

POLLY. Is Mat targeting her?

SILAS. Mat is a planet. Probably in God Mode right now, clocking us.

POLLY. Lin addresses Congress today. Is Sunlight vulnerable?

SILAS. To what?

POLLY. Right to the Dark. Actual touch. Actual connection.

SILAS. Hey hey.

POLLY. Paper zines, picnics on the LowLow, food from the ground. Lin is popular.

SILAS. The endowed chair behind casement windows at a U with a four percent acceptance rate? Popular as in "of the peeps"?

POLLY. Lin is epic.

SILAS. Sunlight will launch Lin's Tale. That's unstoppable.

POLLY. You don't even know her.

SILAS. Mat can do it his way...

POLLY. What's "his way"?

SILAS. Or we can partner for the inside track. Raise your authentic sister. Texture, feels. Truth.

POLLY. The "Tale of the Dark."

SILAS. What's your access?

POLLY. I am her sister. I live in her home.

SILAS. What's that like?

POLLY. I mean, quiet. She works a lot. Shrouded in mystery.

SILAS. And her office? The Enclave?

POLLY. I should go.

SILAS. I told you my parents were immigrants? Also, Underforce.

POLLY. Whoa. How did / they (get there)?

SILAS. What did they do?

POLLY. Oh I don't assume they did – the whole sys/tem –

SILAS. Uh uh uh! Driver's seat!

POLLY. I don't even know where to –

(**SILAS** *keeps it light.*)

SILAS. They started a business! Tech Repair! Took out a loan! Expanding right before Pause Five, when the law flipped to –

POLLY. Debt Redemption via Labor.

SILAS. That right there. One minute we're at the kitchen table puzzling out how to make payroll, and the next minute sirens, a crew at the door, Mom and Pop get pulled to the basement and branded for Underforce.

POLLY. Oh Silas.

SILAS. Clock ran out!

POLLY. Are your folks still –

SILAS. Nearly redeemed!

POLLY. Whoa. What are the odds?

SILAS. Two percent. I owe Mat everything. Raised Underforce since age ten and I'm full time at Sunlight! Anything is possible.

(**POLLY**'s *Sunplant pings.*)

I'm authorized to back you for that amount right now.

(**POLLY** *checks her Sunplant, as if she's reading something behind her eyes. The amount is a lot. The agreement is long.*)

POLLY. Wow, generous. But I don't care about –

SILAS. You're not a resource person, you're a connection person. Me too. But no shame in needing upfront funds. Most Talent Workers do. Advance vests on delivery.

POLLY. Delivery of what?

SILAS. It's all in the agreement.

POLLY. Oh, um – It's what, a thousand pages, so I should review it with my lawyer.

SILAS. A hundred percent.

> (**POLLY** *reads. Obviously she doesn't have a fucking lawyer.*)

When I think about my family, my precious family, if power came for them, I would want to interpret. I would use my talent to shine their truth. I wouldn't leave them exposed to invasive procedures, bad actors –

POLLY. Bad actors like, cringe, or like, evil?

SILAS. That's what I'm saying. So much is unknown.

> (*At no point does* **SILAS** *sound sinister.*)

You can read the small font; that's your right. But life is who you are plus how you meet your time. Now is the time of Sunlight.

POLLY. What happens to Lin if I don't sign?

SILAS. We alone can secure our family legacies.

POLLY. Not betrayal, protection. Amplification.

SILAS. YAS. What does she share that folks need so badly? What is the residue, the felt experience of Lin's course? And what about the breathy touchy drugs?

POLLY. Drugs?

SILAS. We hear she parties.

POLLY. Sure, but so ethically.

SILAS. See, we have our info but you get personal. Raw. You went right to the heart, warming up. Thus the extra zero.

POLLY. I see it. My Debtor's Badge covers my whole back.

SILAS. Girl same. I just started making Sun Money. Full body clear is the Goal. But, priorities.

POLLY. If I bite does it help your folks?

SILAS. Don't think about me; think about you. Where you want to be, what you want to build. Personally? I did a hard capture of my skills, and my dreams, and my actual options in the world as it exists, and at a certain point you say...

POLLY. Yes.

>(**POLLY** *"bites" to sign the document, a short sharp move.*)

SILAS. Big feels.

POLLY. What did I just –

SILAS. Today is a good day.

Scene Two

*(Same day. Lin's old-fashioned Ivy League type office. **LIN**, elegantly dressed, faces us, addressing Congress via a camera we don't see. **LIN** is confident, mesmerizing, the visible emotion of a leader.)*

*(**JACE**, in something like green hair and a kilt, watches **LIN** admiringly, off camera but visible to us.)*

LIN. You gather again. Only together can we explore our right to gather, one of several rights at stake today. Thank you for seeking my counsel.

You meet as an elected governing body, with power still imbued by the people. Use it.

I hope you can see me, through these old fashioned fiber-optics. I meant to join you personally. I have been barred. I have no Sunplant. No one may enter Congress without a Sunplant.

Why?

Sunlight didn't create that policy; you did.

But who benefits?

Weeks ago we learned of "Sunlight Seedbank," a plan to use human cell memory to make so-called "Seedbank Tales," for profit and entertainment.

Did you know that Sunlight harvested cells when you received your free Sunplant?

No. Just as we did not foresee decades ago that early tech companies would mine our images, movements, voices, and feelings as data.

Consider Sunlight's prototype, the AwareHome. Introduced without warning.

Some of you were in office. You imagined how AwareHome might boost happy families. But unhappy families employ the controls too: abusers blasting heat, or refusing heat, engaging locks remotely, making home life a hell without laying a hand.

We barely glanced when Sunlight swallowed AwareHome, expanded to workplaces and prisons. Formalized the Underforce: legal indentured servitude.

At every turn, Sunlight dances between laws: privacy, free speech, medical ethics, research protection, so that you can't even form a committee to stop it.

And now they scrape and sell our memories?

Enough!

Even an underfunded, fractious, and – forgive me – complacent legislature must act.

We never know what Sunlight will try next, but we must understand what we have to lose.

Hold hands.

JACE. YES Congress holding hands!

LIN & JACE. (**LIN** *to Congress,* **JACE** *under breath, knowing the routine.*) Now squeeze. Release. Feel a pulse.

LIN. Breathe together. Settle your bodies. You and I can still remember how.

I'd like you to meet my teaching assistant, a remarkable young leader. Jace?

> (**LIN** *extends a hand.* **JACE** *joins* **LIN**, *facing the camera we can't see.*)

> (**LIN** *might place a comforting hand on* **JACE**'s *shoulder.*)

> (*In contrast to* **LIN**, **JACE** *reads from notes, nervous but gaining confidence.*)

JACE. My name is Jace. I am twenty-three years old.

I am the youth leader of Right to the Dark.

Right to the Dark is a collective movement to rebuild natural alone behavior. To grow back our capacity for full live attention. To know who we are when no one is watching.

I received my Sunplant at age fifteen. My younger sibs received theirs at ages nine, six, and four.

Although the Sunplant is supposed to keep us safe, something else happened.

Sunplant gives directions to all of our destinations – and now our cognitive mapping, the compass in our brains, has shrunk.

Sunplant tells us when to eat, and now we don't know when we're hungry.

Many of us cannot carry out basic tasks without Sunplant. This supposed "convenience" has made us dependent.

We are angry.

But we have hope.

In Right to the Dark, we follow Professor Lin's simple methods of breath and touch.

We pay attention to one another.

We share memories; we tell stories.

We earn and learn intimacy.

And we block our Sunplants in order to do this work.

That is legal. Sunplant is supposed to be optional.

But now Seedbank Tales threaten everything.

By stealing our cells to take memories and stories by force, Seedbank Tales cross a final line. Not just changing our bodies and brains, but *taking* our bodies and brains.

Seedbank Tales would spread our memories, against our will.

Seedbank Tales would make blocking Sunplants useless, because Sunlight has our cells.

Our Sunplants could dictate not only nutrition, and direction, but love and friendship.

Seedbank Tales would end our Right to the Dark.

We who received Sunplants as children did not give consent.

We deserve control over memory and meaning.

Pass an emergency order to end Sunlight Seedbank today!

LIN. That was perfect. Thank you Jace.

> (**JACE**, *relieved, steps out of the camera view.*)

I can take questions now. There is always time for questions. Yes, Representative Pressley.

> (*A technical issue.*)

I'm losing your faces.

I can't read your room.

> (*A bright light goes out, Lin's camera.*)

Dammit! Did we lose the signal?

JACE. I can troubleshoot.

LIN. You know what? You have a Sunplant. Get to Congress. Go in person.

JACE. Me?

LIN. You're ready.

JACE. I'm not. I could try to get you an exemption? There's precedent I think.

LIN. Good. Go.

(*The door opens.* **POLLY** *enters. Surprised to see* **JACE**.)

POLLY. Hey Sis! Um hi…

JACE. You must be Polly.

POLLY. Uh yeah. How was Congress?

LIN. In process. Camera issues.

POLLY. Camera. Whoa, vintage.

JACE. We use our own network. Professor Lin won't Sun Up.

POLLY. Steampunk!

(*Maybe* **POLLY** *thumbs up and* **JACE** *and* **LIN** *don't really care.*)

JACE. (*To* **LIN**.) Back ASAP.

LIN. Jace, you are gold.

(**JACE** *goes.*)

POLLY. You've got fans! Jace. The crowd in the hall…

LIN. Wait list. They'll all sleep here.

POLLY. Icon!

LIN. I'll open new sections. I don't do scarcity.

POLLY. Do you need to go?

LIN. I need to wait for Jace and this exemption.

How was your meeting, Baby Sis?

POLLY. They want me.

> (**LIN** *loses it with high-octane big sister whoops, daps, and cheers. She might pick* **POLLY** *up or do a happy dance around her.*)

LIN. YES THEY DO! Because you're gifted and fiery and an irresistible vector of slay!

POLLY. I'm glad you're happy for me.

LIN. Of course! This was what, a first interview, a –

POLLY. Hired me on the spot.

LIN. YOU STELLAR MOTHERFUCKER.

POLLY. Right? Do you want tea?

LIN. It's too warm. Maybe just water?

POLLY. I'll get it.

LIN. Kettle's there.

> (**POLLY** *pours water from the electric kettle into a mug and gives it to* **LIN**.*)*

POLLY. Wow, check the airflow in here, love the leaded glass.

LIN. I'm a lucky bitch.

POLLY. I shoulda come sooner.

LIN. You're here now.

POLLY. You deserve. You. Deserve. Dismissed at every turn, yet here you are, government expert, Oprah adjacent. With a name, a perch, an Endowed Chair; is there literally a chair?

LIN. Yeah I fart on the leathery gifts of old white men. And now *you* have a gig! I am so proud of you.

POLLY. Really?

LIN. You are going to murder this job! This will unPause you. I see it! You are gonna turn the ship around and FLOURISH!

POLLY. Yay!

LIN. Where was the meeting?!!

> (**POLLY** *hesitates.*)

POLLY. We're not InLight?

LIN. Nope. Enclave.

> (**POLLY** *whispers in* **LIN**'s *ear anyway.* **LIN** *is gutted.*)

No.

POLLY. Yeah?

LIN. Have you read one word of my books?

POLLY. Have you looked at the world? Where did you think I was meeting?

LIN. I don't know.

POLLY. Where else is there?

LIN. I assumed –

POLLY. I don't know if you noticed, but my skillset is extinct. I haven't worked in four years. There is nothing but Sunlight.

LIN. You must be patient.

POLLY. SHUT UP! You're an ethics professor don't just fucking yell at me! Sorry.

LIN. No, no, let's process the ethics.

POLLY. I don't wanna.

LIN. I'm trying to pull Congress together, and you barrel in with pretty upsetting news so pardon me.

POLLY. It gets worse, but also better.

LIN. How?

POLLY. I mentioned my sister and this guy Silas dropped your name.

LIN. Why bring me into it?

POLLY. You were part of my story.

LIN. Did you not think they'd hire you on your merits?

POLLY. Merits. Oh we're there.

LIN. I take it back. Go on.

POLLY. They want to launch a Seedbank Tale about Right to the Dark. You are like the alpha, or the beta? of the Tales.

LIN. Oh no.

POLLY. But. There is an opportunity. For me...to Seed your Tale, your way. Take power for *us*.

LIN. I have power.

POLLY. God you're a shitty sister even when you're a great sister! But let's take you to the people. Not scraped data. Not pirated AI. Real wisdom, real work. If this has to happen, let's make it authentic. Craft the version you want to share, before they drop spies to build out some avatar –

LIN. Did he say avatar? Are you the avatar? Younger and white, that tracks.

POLLY. They're obsessed!

LIN. You met Mat?

POLLY. Silas.

LIN. Who is Silas?

POLLY. Silas is either very important or not at all important?

LIN. If Mat comes for me, so be it. But stay out of this, Polly.

POLLY. Do you want your theories to reach people, or just like your cape and a slogan?

LIN. I publish.

POLLY. "Books."

LIN. Books are stable.

POLLY. What about the ninety percent with only InLight learning; don't you care about them?

LIN. My alumni spread the living message.

POLLY. What are you, Jesus?

LIN. I have students; they have students. Together we mobilize. We amass underground distribution.

POLLY. Slowly.

LIN. I teach Right to the Dark. It makes no sense InLight.

POLLY. Snob.

LIN. Jesus was not a snob.

POLLY. Messiah Complex Elitist Ivy Paywall Snob.

LIN. The revolution will not be Lit.

POLLY. And it won't be tenured.

LIN. I still have a chance with Congress.

POLLY. Ooh "Congress." Oldies vote in "Elections" and now I go to "Congress" where I shape "Laws."

LIN. Laws still matter.

POLLY. "Laws boom but don't block, like thunder chasing lightning."

LIN. You read my book!

POLLY. It was a meme.

LIN. Why don't you study, Polly? You're highly intelligent.

POLLY. I studied.

LIN. You "trained."

POLLY. That hurts my feelings.

LIN. I don't want to hurt you.

POLLY. Your optics are unparalleled. You cared for my mom at the end. *You* cared for *my* mom.

LIN. Reyna was good to me.

POLLY. You're vulnerable.

LIN. I'm barely visible.

POLLY. Get more visible to be less vulnerable.

LIN. Polly polly polly.

POLLY. Shine your brand. A righteous wizard. Potent small fry.

Sunlight can't hurt you with the world watching –

LIN. So you're my hero?

POLLY. Why not me?

LIN. You think you can outsmart *him*? Fight *him*?

POLLY. You do.

LIN. Different.

POLLY. Are ya better than me or just smarter?

LIN. I know it's been hard, but we are back, and the long road belongs to you. You're young.

POLLY. I'm not that young.

LIN. Hunker with me a while longer.

POLLY. I can move out! I got my upfront funds!

(*Beat.*)

LIN. You bit an agreement.

POLLY. Maybe.

LIN. Did you read it?

POLLY. It was too long?

LIN. May I see the agreement?

> (**POLLY** *checks her Sunplant by tapping the same part of her face or neck that Mat tapped earlier.*)

POLLY. It's gone.

LIN. We have to assume you collateralized.

POLLY. What's that?

LIN. They pay an advance, and you stake your labor. If you fail they take you for Underforce.

POLLY. Whoops.

LIN. May I access your Sunplant?

> (**POLLY** *gives access.* **LIN** *scans the document, same gestures* **POLLY** *made, but finds nothing.*)

Sometimes the signee surrenders the right to review.

POLLY. I agreed that I can't read the agreement?

LIN. You are entrapped.

POLLY. Sorry.

LIN. That's not shameful, it's standard. What exactly did you sell?

POLLY. I claimed to know you? Like a sister?

LIN. So I need to make that true. This will be fun. I have a reading list –

POLLY. Books?

LIN. Yes books.

POLLY. I just thought it would be excellent to know you you.

LIN. Oh.

POLLY. I'm dumb.

LIN. No you're brilliant. I love you more than life.

POLLY. Same.

LIN. We don't know your timeline, but Mat moves fast. I'll help you.

POLLY. No no no! This isn't Lin Saves Polly Episode 93. It has to be win-win.

LIN. I need a message out; you have a platform. Let's partner.

POLLY. Serious?

LIN. Just enough to meet the minimum deliverable. Think of it as a research project.

POLLY. Sure.

LIN. We'll stay with what has been published. The materials I wish to share anyway. When InLight learning erased libraries, people lost basic history. Your "Tale" can restore that. Win-win.

POLLY. I think we can do this without taking your cells.

LIN. We are definitely doing this without taking my cells.

POLLY. I need to help others feel like you. Magnetic. Connected. Whole. Who are you? What inspired Right to the Dark?

> (**LIN** *thinks.*)

LIN. Have you ever been alone with another person, outdoors, and no one had a device?

POLLY. No.

LIN. Okay, new example. When I was a baby, I had no monitor.

POLLY. *What?*

LIN. Dad was a broke-ass student, and my mom stayed home.

POLLY. How did they sleep?

LIN. They paid attention. Even at rest.

POLLY. Mama baby spidey sense.

LIN. Everyone my age and older fed on that gaze, as infants.

Mirroring. Live and private.

Then you had a monitor, but it was a closed loop.

POLLY. What's a closed loop?

      (**LIN** *sighs.*)

Don't be a dick about it.

LIN. *(Bedtime story.)* In the twentieth century, there were land lines.

POLLY. I know about land lines.

LIN. Great then you're set.

POLLY. Shut up.

LIN. In early prototypes, human women plugged wires into jacks in central hubs. These women were termed "operators" and they physically connected the calls.

POLLY. With their hands?

LIN. Yes.

POLLY. So before technology.

LIN. It was technology.

POLLY. But you said people plugged things in.

LIN. Fabric is technology. Wires are technology. Technology is any artifice of civilization.

POLLY. Did the "operators" listen?

LIN. Sometimes. But the phone company did not capture conversations.

POLLY. Why?

LIN. Well they couldn't. Recording was analog, unscannable, so there was no way to store and sell it. Plus there was a cultural ethos –

POLLY. A what?

LIN. A shared moral understanding that the phone company carried the voices, without rights to the content.

POLLY. Then how did they profit?

LIN. It cost a lot to use the phone. You paid direct.

POLLY. Then what was "wiretapping"?

LIN. *(Smart question!)* Wiretapping was *spying*. By the *government*. A big deal.

POLLY. How could the *government* afford access?

LIN. The government paid to develop surveillance in the first place. It was not for private use. In fact a president was impeached for wiretapping other candidates.

POLLY. *(Nixon gesture.)* Nixon!

LIN. Good girl.

POLLY. So users shared audio data –

LIN. Not data, no byproduct. Just voice, cable, and the ear.

POLLY. They talked –

LIN. Yeah –

POLLY. Through a web of –

LIN. Encased copper wires. In the Outer Plains you still see the poles.

POLLY. And no one captured anything? That is wild.

LIN. Conversations went unknown and untraced, like meeting in person on a mountain. There was a deep privacy, a shadow.

POLLY. Democracy dies in darkness.

LIN. But that's not how it died.

> *(Beat.)*

POLLY. You hold your mug with both hands. That's cozy.

LIN. Any questions?

POLLY. Yeah, what the fuck does this have to do with you?

LIN. It is our history.

POLLY. But what's the hook?

LIN. Oh good god.

POLLY. You want to like, take us backwards, to wires?

> *(**LIN** is silent.)*

Jk jk. You want to like, be our own baby monitors. Grow back the mama baby spidey sense?

LIN. Not wrong.

POLLY. Did you ever want kids?

LIN. Meh, I meet youth every year. I'll be boss Auntie when you harvest. I should find Jace.

POLLY. What's up with your drugs?

LIN. Oh the dosing.

POLLY. Silas says you party. But you're like the opposite of a party.

LIN. Each year I enroll students who got their Sunplants at a younger age. The Sunplant impedes the development of their bearings, so that breath and touch no longer suffice as tools to build the inner self. They are anxious. They lack access. Jace proposed a controlled substance to help reset clarity. I got licensed, of course. Consent. Disclosure.

POLLY. You even make it boring to get high.

LIN. Is it warm or is it me?

POLLY. It's warm. You're perfect.

        *(**LIN** and **POLLY** shed layers.)*

LIN. What you endured Pause by Pause, all of the Talent Workers.

It's been brutal. Of course you went to Sunlight. We'll solve it, Sis.

        *(**POLLY** imitates **LIN**'s address. She's uncanny.)*

POLLY. Grab a pencil. Disconnect. Note harms.

Harm occurs when you shut off possibility because your future is determined.

Breathe with others. Form physical groups.

Technology is analog.

Technology is warp and weft.

Technology is thread.

LIN. Yes!

Make your Tale.

You're right. We must act.

I lack sufficient reach.

LIN. People are in despair. They are sick, they are broke, they chase medicine, shelter, even food. In this nation with the surplus and the Workfarms, *people chase food.*

I'm a tenured professor without kids. The U provides a townhome.

POLLY. Maybe hush on the free home...

LIN. If we can't be brave, who can?

Here are my notebooks, course plans, files.

POLLY. Vintage.

LIN. Read, gather, discover, convey.

Let's do this.

POLLY. Is it hotter?

LIN. Yeah, let me show you how to turn down the –

(**LIN** *goes to the radiator.*)

It's off.

POLLY. Should we check the –

(**LIN** *checks the thermostat.*)

LIN. A hundred and twelve.

POLLY. Let's get out of here.

(*The loud click of a lock.*)

Scan your eye.

LIN. This office is not Aware.

POLLY. Then how do you lock it?

LIN. With a key. Jace?

(**LIN** *tries the door. They are locked in.*)

POLLY. How do you control the heat?

LIN. Radiator.

POLLY. Serious?

LIN. But it's off.

POLLY. Then what is warming?

LIN. We must be Lit. Sunlight is here.

> (**LIN** *addresses her students the way she spoke to Congress.*)

Right to the Dark TAs, alumni, students and fans:

I'm speaking from what I thought was the Enclave.

If I am Lit, so are you.

POLLY. Is that like a *landline camera*?

LIN. What's next? We decide.

Sunlight is not human, but we are.

POLLY. Rogue.

LIN. If we lose contact, make contact.

Trust each other.

Oldies broke the earth but there is open space.

There's no surveillance in the Outer Plains.

Be your own leaders.

Use the tools at hand.

POLLY. Let's use the chair. Break a window.

LIN. Yes.

> (*The sisters lift the heavy chair. They are about to swing it through Lin's window when the locked door opens.*)

Thank god. Jace?

(**SILAS** *enters.*)

SILAS. Hey.

(**LIN** *and* **POLLY** *stand staring at* **SILAS**. *They are partially undressed and sweating. It's like he's in a sitcom and they are in a horror film, but playing along.*)

POLLY. Silas!

SILAS. Just checking on progress. It's been a minute.

POLLY. Like literally a minute.

SILAS. Mat's pretty eager. You've got that first deliverable.

POLLY. I do?

SILAS. Turns out!

LIN. Who made it hot in here?

SILAS. Did you check your – (radiator)

LIN. YES.

SILAS. Weird.

LIN. How long has my Enclave been Aware?

SILAS. Oh I'm not at that level. This is my first time at the U.

She's pretty.

LIN. Malicious use of AwareHome is a felony.

SILAS. I'm sorry for your discomfort.

Polly, how 'bout you show me the boiler room and we'll get to the bottom of this?

POLLY. The boiler room...

SILAS. You know the building!

POLLY. Sure.

LIN. I'll go.

SILAS. Great!

LIN. *(To **POLLY**.)* Wait here until Jace comes back.

SILAS. But if you help, Professor, that's a fail for Polly.

LIN. Ah.

POLLY. Don't hate the playa hate the game!

LIN. Why are you in this game? Why did you go to Sunlight? I support you. I take care of you.

POLLY. I WANT TO BE AN ADULT!

SILAS. Polly and I are a team. I'm gonna redeem my fam and she's gonna pay her ladybank before they repurpose her eggs.

LIN. You missed a payment?

POLLY. Hi I'm Polly, I have nothing.

LIN. Why does Silas know?

POLLY. Silas asks good questions!

LIN. Reyna left you *one thing,* and all you had to do was maintain payments –

POLLY. Why do you care?

LIN. Because you want a family!

POLLY. Maybe I'll be like you and start a cult instead!

SILAS. I always wanted a sister, but I pictured it different.

LIN. Do not leave this office.

POLLY. I can handle myself.

> (**SILAS** *and* **POLLY** *go.)*

> *(Beat. The door swings open.)*

> (**MAT** *enters. Bright energy.)*

MAT. Knock knock!

LIN. What have you done with my sister.

MAT. Miles discovered her! They have a project! Juicy stuff! We hope she delivers.

LIN. You broke the Enclave. You made this office Aware.

MAT. You were my favorite professor.

Your Ethics and the Future class blew my mind.

LIN. Let's go.

MAT. You're protective. How sweet. But –

(Mmm sound.)

Can you really rescue Polly? Or will you just wreck her chances?

LIN. I believe utterly in my sister.

*(**LIN** closes the door.)*

MAT. There is an order to things.

And good news: that order includes you. Your voice, your plans, your badass legitimacy. Your Enclave, your dosing, your buzzy intuition. Your touch.

All I want to do is celebrate you. Just affirm all you made possible.

You made me.

And although your estrogen levels have dropped, I hope there's enough maternal chemistry to beam upon the shift.

I need you. Let that feel good.

Are you sweating, Professor?

LIN. It was a hundred and twelve degrees.

MAT. You run hot internally.

LIN. I have no Sunplant. You can't read my bio.

MAT. We own the waste water here so I know you take supplements and I know they're not working.

LIN. It makes you look weak and skeevy to manhandle my biodata.

People hate you for spying on our literal shit.

MAT. But they can't look away.

LIN. And now cells.

MAT. The cells are just a path.

LIN. To more power?

MAT. Not at all. To –

(Chef's kiss – "so close.")

Back in the day, you made me feel some kinda way, some kinda close. I want to share that with the world.

LIN. Seedbank's not working, is it?

MAT. It's a process.

LIN. I think you stole our cells, resurrected them, and found nothing but a pile of data. So you hire people like my sister to make meaning from the memory swarm. To build Tales. To deliver the commodity of Close. But let me guess. You're still lonely.

MAT. I have a perfect fam.

LIN. You remind me of the boy titan who sent himself to space.

MAT. Fuck space. I want less space. I want to be up in each other's hearts and minds. You're the expert. You're the intimacy goddess. Except maybe with your sister.

LIN. Where's Polly?

MAT. That's up to her.

This office is so artisanal. I always loved it. Gothic.

LIN. Fake Gothic, but built during the First Depression when labor –

MAT. Was cheap –

LIN. Labor was hurting, Mat, and it was a social good to commission intricate ironwork. Pretentious, but ethical.

MAT. So we're waiting for Sis? We're chatting?

LIN. So far.

MAT. We connect we connect we connect. And so can you. You matter.

LIN. I know.

MAT. Where do you get your confidence?

LIN. Thirty years of study and six books. Where do you get yours?

MAT. I always knew I had more to offer others than they had to offer me.

LIN. Yet you wish to animate a version of me in your first Seedbank Tale. Why?

MAT. *(Pictures on Lin's desk.)* Same photos. No kids?

LIN. You know I don't have kids.

MAT. Just the abortion.

LIN. I'm published on that point so shame is not a tool available to you.

MAT. Are you happy with your choice?

LIN. I'm glad I had the choice. That was a better system.

MAT. In which pregnant people could hide their status and use their own moral metrics to decide?

LIN. Yeah that was better.

MAT. You terminated early.

LIN. Please exit my office.

MAT. But not right when you found out. You waited.

LIN. It was a process.

MAT. Do you feel regret?

LIN. A certain counterfactual loop.

MAT. That sounds sad.

LIN. And here, Mat, lies the thrill of intimate ethics. Clarity is not a hundred percent possible nor measurable. So we train the moral apparatus to parse hard decisions. That's Right to the Dark.

MAT. *Restore the Guilt.* I loved that book.

LIN. "Who am I when no one is watching?"

MAT. Are ya guilty? Are you ashamed?

LIN. I am ashamed of you. I am ashamed that you dredge my work and cite my course as ballast for your greedy shaky empire. And I hope you are ashamed of yourself.

MAT. I'm not ashamed of myself, "Mom."

LIN. I don't feel maternal towards you. I don't even care about you.

MAT. Ouch.

LIN. But you care what I think.

MAT. You're my North Star.

We want the same thing. Front row seats to each other's truth.

LIN. Then why does your family have a shield?

MAT. People love to hate a first family. They deserve to be kids.

LIN. *Your* twins deserve to be kids, unobserved?

MAT. If you were a mom you might understand.

LIN. All young people need refuge. Not just yours.

MAT. Sunlight will host Right to the Dark.

LIN. That's facially impossible.

MAT. I bought the university.

> *(Beat.)*

LIN. Bullshit.

MAT. Times are tough. And I was curious.

LIN. We have a forty billion dollar endowment.

MAT. Nonprofit model doesn't work.

LIN. It has worked four hundred years.

MAT. Exactly, this place was founded before women could vote, using slave trade profits. It's immoral.

LIN. There is a plan for reparations.

MAT. That was never gonna happen.

LIN. This generation is smart. They are kind. They want to support each other, mutual support.

MAT. We'll see.

LIN. We're unprofitable; leave us alone.

MAT. You're the avatar. I need you.

LIN. Why?

MAT. Folks love you. They compete to be in rooms with you. I bet they still try to sleep with you.

LIN. So?

MAT. They market tacky crap with your face and slogans, tattoo your icons onto their arms, but no one knows you. You've kept yourself scarce, real, that's a brand.

LIN. Reality is not a brand.

MAT. It is tho. That's why it has an acronym, IRL.

LIN. You can't verticalize me. You can't synthesize me. You can't change the basic need to connect.

MAT. I own the need to connect.

LIN. You tipped too far and now people hate you. You're losing the young. As soon as they learn about the LowLow, they are done being watched. Natural and free.

MAT. In your teeny tiny lab with your A plus plus students. Sure, spread the LowLow but there will be more plague, more Pauses, more light.

LIN. Take me to Polly.

(Hideous sirens, close by.)

MAT. Polly didn't work out.

LIN. **Where's my sister?**

MAT. Miles took her to scope the boiler but she couldn't even find it.

(Sirens again.)

LIN. That girl has been through a lot, she just lost her mom, bring back that girl.

MAT. Polly's not a baby. She's an adult.

LIN. Call back your crew!

MAT. Why would I do that?

LIN. Release Polly.

MAT. She didn't deliver.

LIN. She just signed.

MAT. And she already failed to add value. She doesn't know you at all.

LIN. She has the knack.

MAT. You never let her in. Why?

LIN. I do let her in.

MAT. You write books she doesn't read. You wait for her to find you. Do you think she's a baby? Do you think she's your baby? Do you miss your baby?

   (**LIN** *slaps* **MAT**'s *face.*)

LIN. Polly taught me how to be a person.

   (**SILAS** *and* **POLLY** *enter.* **POLLY** *has been burned or branded in a shocking way.*)

You're branded for Underforce.

Let's get you care.

   (**SILAS** *and* **POLLY** *are shook, but cover with a bright manic flair.*)

POLLY. Nuh uh no.

SILAS. We're making a Thing!

POLLY. Will you help? Please please please!

LIN. *(To* **MAT**.*)* Show me her agreement.

MAT. We're assessing Polly's role. Miles claims she can craft a Tale.

LIN. Your name is Silas.

SILAS. I'm good with whatevs.

POLLY. It turns out I overpromised? I'm not a clear channel? But Silas says I have potential.

   (**LIN** *regards* **SILAS** *with full, gentle attention.*)

LIN. Silas?

   (He opens.)

SILAS. Professor Lin.

LIN. My sister walked out of this office intact, with you.

POLLY. *(Still chipper.)* It wasn't him! It was a crew! I signed! I fucked up. Rules are rules!

LIN. *(To **SILAS**.)* How did you become loyal to Sunlight?

POLLY. Silas is exceptional. He is working off his parents' debt. He has like one bonus to go!

LIN. Silas, that must have been a hard way to grow up.

SILAS. I'm all good.

LIN. You don't need to accommodate violence in order to belong.

> *(**LIN** and **SILAS** breathe together.)*

It makes you cruel.

> *(**LIN** and **SILAS** breathe together.)*

It makes you hate yourself.

> *(**LIN** and **SILAS** breathe together.)*

You deserve to love yourself.

> *(**LIN** and **SILAS** breathe together. Then **SILAS** breaks away brightly.)*

SILAS. I love my job, Mat! I am so fortunate to be up here. I was telling Polly how good it is up here.

POLLY. Yeah I really really want to stay up here. I want to get my skin back. Lin, let me know you. Let me in. I gotta get you, I gotta show you, I gotta make something real.

LIN. *(To **MAT**.)* Why not put *this* InLight? Brutality and mutilation?

Capriciousness and dread? The flesh and blood grind fueling Sunlight?

MAT. If Polly delivers, her conversion is temporary. So go ahead to Congress. Rock the vote.

LIN. I'll wait.

SILAS. Sunlight doesn't shadow. We shine the bright light of truth!

MAT. But why her?

POLLY. Me?

MAT. We purchased access to an epic hero. What is the access?

LIN. Polly knows my systems. She knows where I keep my syllabi, my notes.

POLLY. Paper notes! I gotchu Lin.

LIN. Use my office. Open anything. Just give him a Tale and get clear.

POLLY. I can't do that with books.

LIN. Why not?

POLLY. I need more. I need in. I need something to offer. From here.

> *(Her heart.)*

LIN. That was not our agreement. Private memories are –

POLLY. Don't use the word "sacred." I'm stuck.

> *(Beat.)*

LIN. – personal.

POLLY. I want that. Don't you? Don't you want to be known?

LIN. By you, yes.

POLLY. Tell me.

> *(**POLLY** carefully follows **LIN**'s every word.)*

LIN. When I was nineteen my car broke down at night, without a phone. I flagged a stranger. He changed my tire. I gave him a twenty. I drove to a gas station and asked for directions. Another stranger pointed to a paper map: "we are here." I used my gut to judge helpers.

POLLY. I had to pay very careful attention, to the helpers, and the road.

LIN. I did not witness a sexual act until I participated in sex.

SILAS. Wait what?

LIN. The first body with another body was my own. I had no metric of comparison. No images. We just were.

POLLY. I had to pay very careful attention to my lover, and myself.

SILAS. Hot.

MAT. Why? Why is that hot?

SILAS. Nevermind.

MAT. Shine it, Silas.

SILAS. Truth, some of my friend groups are stepping away from Sunlight, seeking that private thrill. Which is why Seedbank Tales will be so win-win.

MAT. How are your agemates cutting out?

SILAS. They do these Just Us dinners – leave devices, block Sunplants, roam with food. Eat Just Us. It's big with tweens and emerging adults.

MAT. Outside?

SILAS. Naw, too hard to breathe, but the goal is darkness, the LowLow. No one knows what Lin does exactly, but they... *(Looks for word.)* explore. Experience.

MAT. We can do that. We can vibe that. We're all about search. You say no one *knows* the real Lin but now we can offer that.

POLLY. I'm your girl.

MAT. You taught Lin how to be a person.

POLLY. Hells yeah.

>   (**POLLY** *glances at* **LIN**, *come on, help me!*)

LIN. When you were a baby, I watched you for hours, sometimes days or weeks.

POLLY. You did?

LIN. Oh god it was slow. I sang you songs from Dad's Bruce Springsteen album, American folk about rising up, oh my god, you couldn't talk. We just gazed and smiled and patted and bopped. Oh god I was bored, oh god I adored you, watching shadows change on the wall, just us.

POLLY. You had to pay very careful attention, to me.

LIN. Your first word was a sentence, "Dat's ok!" We… between the diapers and the cooking I forgot to clean and there were suddenly…*ants*! Everywhere! Armies of ants and I'm uselessly sweeping but that just scatters the battalions, so I start stamping the floor, mangling the ants, and the dishes are filthy and you are filthy and the phone's ringing off the wall and you stamp into the middle of the mess, with me, and yell *"Dat's ok!"*

POLLY. This was before the lover? Before the car breakdown?

LIN. Yeah, I was in middle school. I didn't know I had it in me, to be there for someone? To be resourceful? To pay attention? I felt like a superhero but also, a person. This is what it is to be a person. I was such a nerd. I didn't have friends. I didn't know how. You gave me that.

POLLY. "Dat's ok!"

LIN. "Dat's ok!"

POLLY. We were besties!

LIN. We were.

POLLY. Where was my mom?

LIN. Reyna was... maybe she was the one calling.

POLLY. My mom was gone for *weeks*?

>   (**LIN** *didn't mean to admit that.*)

LIN. Maybe a week, here and there.

>   (*Beat.*)

She checked in. There was money, there were supplies.

POLLY. You were in *middle school*?

LIN. I was highly / responsible.

POLLY. Responsible.

Where was Dad?

LIN. At the lab a lot, and...also after.

>   (**POLLY** *remembers something.*)

POLLY. Was there a bad phone call? On the land line?

LIN. Yeah.

POLLY. Is that how you learned about Dad?

LIN. Yeah.

POLLY. Just us?

LIN. I couldn't give you the news. Obviously.

POLLY. You were watching me. But who was watching you?

LIN. That's a big question.

>   (*Tiny beat.* **MAT** *cuts in brightly.*)

MAT. Dig there.

POLLY. Sure!

MAT. That's what we want to feel.

POLLY. Tender.

MAT. Besties.

POLLY. I wish I remembered better.

MAT. It's not too late. You can find more.

SILAS. YAAS you can.

POLLY. *(To* **LIN.***)* Sit with me? Talk to me?

> *(But instead,* **LIN** *unlocks file cabinets and drawers, maybe an old-timey secret compartment. Gathers papers and books, perhaps odd spiritual icons as well as academic material.)*

LIN. I'm here. I'm in here. And right there. All you have to do is look.

POLLY. This is you?

LIN. Take notes, journals, sketches. A lifetime of work. If you cross reference you can build something out, something true, a moment in time. My work is me.

(**POLLY** *dives into Lin's material.)*

MAT. Care made you a person. Fire.

LIN. If we don't care for one another we devolve. Care bestows the capacity to witness. To hold one another through helplessness.

MAT. Like me with my twins.

LIN. Like you with your twins. The Pause restored something.

MAT. It did! But hour by hour. Year by year. I mean...

SILAS. I understand pets! I never understood pets!

LIN. I.e., why would you burden yourself on purpose?

SILAS. For love! For care! To feel those feels!

MAT. Everyone deserves feels, even folks who can't afford kids.

LIN. There is so much wrong with that sentence.

MAT. Lin, your long mornings won't be boring in the Tale. A Seedbank Tale is a memory, but better. It's cuddling for just the right amount of time, without hurting your arm. It's taking Baby Sis to the park but there are no unhoused and you don't need sunscreen and the restrooms are spic and span. The phone rings with fun times. It is so...

> *(Chef's kiss: "so close.")*

SILAS. I can't wait.

> *(**LIN** places a hand on **MAT**'s shoulder. Comfortable, professional. He's awkward with it.)*

LIN. When did you buy the University?

MAT. For my fam. It's hard to raise kids on an island they own. BB and Mazz wanted to vibe a real campus. They love romping the halls and quads. So vintage. So safe. Good things happen here.

LIN. Come to class.

MAT. In the Dark?

LIN. Not a one way mirror, but equal footing. Get vintage.

MAT. Are the lights literally off?

LIN. I'm amused you don't know.

Sometimes we just perceive one another in space.

MAT. Meditation! I app'd that.

SILAS. Fave. You select how bored you want to be, and we bling when you need it.

LIN. Sometimes we sit for hours.

Sometimes we feed each other.

Sometimes we close our eyes.

MAT. Sometimes you dose.

LIN. Carefully controlled.

MAT. Could I dose?

LIN. If you give consent, and show physical and emotional stability.

Don't worry Mat, we keep the forms private.

At the end of each session of radical presence, we ask – did something happen here we should fight to protect? Can you, in this institution that primes you to lead, commit to experiential ethics?

MAT. Experiential Ethics. Love.

SILAS. My Just Us dinner friends sense each other, feed each other.

Eating is key.

LIN. Eating is a bug for Sunlight, correct?

SILAS. People don't like to eat alone and they high key don't like to eat alone watching others eat together.

MAT. We will crack that.

LIN. Eating opens boundaries. A habanero pepper in your mouth and in mine – we are biting a tangible, together.

SILAS. Folks crave that.

MAT. Our people eat together!

SILAS. Kind of. We snack. We snack on separate treats.

MAT. *(To* **LIN**.*)* What do you do about gluten?

LIN. We discuss needs. Folks bring fruit.

MAT. That's it? Fucking fruit?

SILAS. My mates will be amazed I met you, Professor. Fruit. That's fire.

LIN. We restore intimacy, and train youth to restore it to others. A hands-on army.

SILAS. Hands-on how?

MAT. Army how?

(**POLLY** *looks up.*)

POLLY. Sis I'm stuck.

LIN. Read faster. Here, can I clarify –

POLLY. It's not enough.

LIN. Use letters. Use diaries. Take it all.

POLLY. I can't read my way out.

I'm gonna need more.

(*Beat.*)

LIN. Fuck.

POLLY. It could be any kind of cell. It doesn't have to hurt.

(*Beat.*)

SILAS. *(Positive.)* This could be monster. You know each other. You love each other. That's been our missing piece? And Polly has a Sunplant, so she'll metabolize fast. Plus with her skills, this could go deep.

LIN. If I refuse?

POLLY. I guess I stay Under.

MAT. Afraid so.

POLLY. Deal's a deal.

> *(Beat.)*
>
> *(**LIN** yanks or snips strands of her own hair. She hands them to **POLLY**.)*

Once I get your memory cells, I'll know how to sort them.

It's the easiest way.

LIN. Easy for you.

> *(**POLLY** swallows **LIN**'s hair.)*
>
> *(She hands a piece to **SILAS** who swallows too.)*
>
> *(**LIN** turns away.)*

POLLY. We're starting the Tale!

SILAS. Polly you got this. Boss, it's the One!

> *(**SILAS** exits to the hall. **POLLY** sits at Lin's desk. She's added an elegant Lin-type clothing element.)*
>
> *(Outside the office, **SILAS** knocks. We are inside the Tale. **SILAS** plays student Mat; **POLLY** plays Lin. It feels realistic and intimate.)*
>
> *(**SILAS** plays student Mat, until indicated.)*

Professor Lin?

> *(**POLLY** plays Lin, until indicated.)*

POLLY. Mat, come in.

> *(Although **POLLY-AS-LIN**'s language seems stern, her tone is warm and compassionate. **SILAS-AS-MAT** is painfully vulnerable.)*

SILAS. I don't know if I need an appointment?

POLLY. That's what office hours are for.

SILAS. Why do people come to office hours?

POLLY. Some people come to discuss the material in greater depth.

Some come with questions about assignments. I'm afraid some come to dispute their grades. But sit down, Mat.

SILAS. I'm in your Ethics of the Future seminar.

POLLY. I know.

SILAS. I'm struggling.

POLLY. How can I help you?

SILAS. I'm really really struggling.

> (**SILAS-AS-MAT** *sobs and shudders, a puppy shaking off water.*)

POLLY. It's tough to be new. You're a transfer student?

SILAS. That's not why.

> (*More shuddering, hard for him to breathe.*)

POLLY. I see.

> (**POLLY-AS-LIN** *hands* **SILAS-AS-MAT** *tissues.*)

SILAS. Can we close the door?

> (**POLLY-AS-LIN** *makes a judgment call and moves to close the door.*)

POLLY. Sure.

SILAS. Can I tell you a secret?

POLLY. Some secrets I can keep. Some I need to report.

SILAS. I don't know what to do, I don't know what to do, I don't know what to do!

> (**SILAS-AS-MAT** *hits his own head several times.*)

POLLY. Poor thing.

> (**SILAS-AS-MAT** *stops.*)

SILAS. What secrets do you keep and what do you need to report?

POLLY. If life is in danger, I need to report. I need to report assault. I need to report sales of illegal drugs. I need to report a suicide risk.

SILAS. My dad died.

POLLY. I'm so sorry.

SILAS. I'm failing.

POLLY. You're not failing my class, you just missed one assignment –

SILAS. I'm so new here, no one would believe me.

POLLY. Of course we believe you.

SILAS. I didn't know how to leave. I didn't – it was way too much –

I didn't have money for a ticket –

POLLY. Can your mom –

SILAS. My mom is a mess!

POLLY. Well sure.

SILAS. I fucked up, I fucked up so bad!

> (*He bangs his head.*)

POLLY. Okay, okay Mat.

(She puts a hand on his shoulder. A professional, comforting touch. He melts.)

SILAS. Why do you love me?

*(***POLLY-AS-LIN*** gently removes her hand.)*

POLLY. I care about students.

SILAS. Why?

POLLY. Growth is tender.

SILAS. You could do anything to me. You could hurt me so bad.

POLLY. I would never.

SILAS. Why?

POLLY. Youth is sacred.

SILAS. Do you believe in God?

POLLY. Not precisely.

SILAS. Same. I'd rather be God.

POLLY. *(Kind.)* What can I do for you, Mat?

SILAS. Should I go to my mom? Should I go to my sister?

POLLY. How would you work out that question?

SILAS. I missed his funeral.

POLLY. Was it sudden?

SILAS. It was self-harm.

POLLY. Oh I'm so sorry.

SILAS. I saw it coming.

POLLY. You couldn't.

SILAS. I knew he was making plans.

POLLY. Your father should not have shared that with you. It's too big a burden, and not yours to carry.

SILAS. I can read his mail.

POLLY. *(Gently.)* That's not possible.

SILAS. I solved his passwords. I know what he ordered. I saw him place the orders. Different sites. Everything legal in each state where he placed the order, in legal quantities, but I saw it together.

POLLY. Oh.

SILAS. Do you need to report that?

POLLY. I don't know.

      *(**SILAS-AS-MAT** bangs his head.)*

I'm going to open the door.

SILAS. Why?

POLLY. Just a little.

      *(**SILAS-AS-MAT** keeps banging his head.)*

SILAS. It's my fault it's my fault it's my fault it's my fault.

      *(On her way to the door, **POLLY-AS-LIN** puts her hand on **SILAS-AS-MAT**'s shoulder. He quiets immediately.)*

POLLY. It's not your fault, Mat.

SILAS. I'm so scared.

      (He holds her hand, pressing it into his shoulder.)

POLLY. I'm going to level with you. I'm not going to bullshit you.

SILAS. Don't bullshit me ever.

POLLY. This is a terrifying big deal. There is no grownup with an answer for you.

You are very young and you have lost your father and you feel responsible. Your life is not over but it's going to change, no matter what you choose.

SILAS. I want to tell you everything.

POLLY. You can tell me what you want. I explained the limits to confidentiality.

> *(She gently extricates her hand and opens the office door a little. He straightens in his chair.)*

SILAS. I like the way you process ethics.

POLLY. You've got more of a four hundred level problem than a 101 problem, huh?

SILAS. Except it's over because he's dead.

POLLY. What questions are active for you?

SILAS. Should I go to my mom and sister?

POLLY. Where are they?

SILAS. Florida.

POLLY. That's not too long a flight.

SILAS. It's all I can think about.

POLLY. Of course it is.

SILAS. But I'm not doing so well, here.

POLLY. Who's the dean of your house?

SILAS. Osinto.

POLLY. I can write him.

SILAS. He'll think I'm weak.

POLLY. Grief is not weak. Grief is human.

SILAS. I barely knew my dad. It shouldn't matter.

POLLY. When you lose a parent, Mat, you lose the dad he was but you also lose the dad he wasn't. The relationship can't grow anymore, and that is hard. It's hard even for adults.

SILAS. I'm twenty.

POLLY. I figured.

SILAS. Should I take the money from his account, for a ticket?

POLLY. Uh.

SILAS. I can't use his AmEx because that terminates with the person.

But the bank account still operates. He has enough.

POLLY. Why don't you consult your mom?

SILAS. I told you my mom is a mess. My sister is nine. It's so fucked up for her. I just want to see her. I should have gone. I couldn't look in their faces and know I knew. I'm so ashamed.

> (**POLLY-AS-LIN** *processes an ethical question in a batshit context.*)

POLLY. Are you the beneficiary on the account?

SILAS. Probably.

POLLY. If you have access to the account, that is something you could ascertain.

SILAS. You don't think I should go.

POLLY. If you are the beneficiary on the account, I believe it's ethical for you to take the funds. If your mother is the beneficiary, you need her consent.

SILAS. My mom has a lover.

POLLY. That's complicated.

SILAS. They are planning to be together.

POLLY. Do you read your mother's email?

SILAS. No one tells me shit!

POLLY. You need to stop reading private correspondence.

SILAS. Dude is garbage. His messages to my mom are like –
violent.

POLLY. That's a difficult situation.

SILAS. Now that I know, I can't unknow. I can't unread
those messages.

POLLY. Mat, you need to level with everybody. You need to
get yourself out of the god position. You don't belong in
the god position.

SILAS. What if he hurts my sister?

POLLY. Right.

SILAS. What did you want for your sister Polly, when your
dad self-harmed?

> *(Weird, but* **POLLY-AS-LIN** *can justify him
> knowing this. She's written about it.)*

POLLY. I wanted Polly to be safe, to know love. Being a big
sib feels enormous, but remember you are her brother,
not her dad.

SILAS. *(A child, a puppy.)* What would you want for your
baby? The one you're gonna have?

> *(***POLLY-AS-LIN** *pauses. Not one soul knows
> she's pregnant.)*

POLLY. Uh.

SILAS. Help me.

POLLY. I have another appointment.

SILAS. No, you blocked this time for research.

POLLY. You need help I can't provide.

SILAS. I read your book. *The Refuge*. I love it. You should get tenure.

POLLY. I'm trying.

SILAS. We need prospect *and* refuge! It's not enough to explore, we need to shelter!

POLLY. I'm going to message Dean Osinto.

SILAS. Do you think I should go?

POLLY. Yes, go now.

SILAS. And face them down? Or table it?

POLLY. Go now, from my office. You can make your own decision about your family. Clearly you have information.

SILAS. You said we must acquire all data to make a decision.

POLLY. All available data.

SILAS. More is available to me. It's right there.

POLLY. How is it right there for you?

SILAS. The codes are so dumb.

POLLY. Mat. You have a gift with code –

SILAS. Thanks!

POLLY. But widen your lens. Consider cultural codes, ethical codes.

The fabric of our agreements. If you break human codes, we can't bear the cost.

SILAS. That's so smart. You helped me so much.

(*He rises.*)

POLLY. I need to consider what to disclose.

SILAS. You're my hero.

(**SILAS-AS-MAT** *leaves, in great spirits.* **POLLY** *speaks brightly as herself.*)

POLLY. And that is the Seedbank Tale of Professor Lin!

MAT. Love!

POLLY. Thank you!

MAT. Silas, you were right about her. Nailed it!

SILAS. *(Entering, as himself.)* Thanks Boss!

MAT. I am pumped for this tale!

SILAS. Thanks man!

MAT. You just slipped on in there.

SILAS. I'm ear to the ground. But Polly's got the goods.

MAT. Indeed.

LIN. Was that her deliverable?

MAT. DELIVERED!

LIN. And her agreement?

MAT. FULFILLED!

POLLY. Great!

LIN. It's over.

MAT. *(**POLLY***'s brand or scar.)* That's gonna heal.

POLLY. Amazing!

MAT. What's it about? Who's the compelling, attractive guy?

SILAS. Who is the guy named *Mat*?

MAT. I have one T. That guy had two.

SILAS. I didn't spell it?

LIN. I'm glad you escaped your jam. Now I'll get to my own affairs. Check on Jace, check on Congress. Excuse me.

POLLY. You were *pregnant*?

LIN. It's in my books.

POLLY. And you just *ended it*?

LIN. You should read me. You would know.

POLLY. Who was the dad?

LIN. Not relevant.

POLLY. Why don't I know *anything*?

LIN. Oh gosh, let me think.

POLLY. I'm your sister. Why do you live like you don't have a sister? Am I nothing? Am I useless?

MAT. On the contrary, you. have. value.

POLLY. Thank you!

MAT. And you, muh dude, are

(*Announcer voice.*) **REDEEMED redeemed** redeemed.

(**SILAS** *glows.*)

SILAS. My parents.

MAT. On their way up!

POLLY. Silas. You did it.

SILAS. My whole family together, Aboveground.

POLLY. Do you want to go tell them?

SILAS. Their balance...

(*Checks via Sunplant.*)

Already cleared. I paid their debt. With my mind. With our idea to – Polly, it was you.

POLLY. I'm just a channel.

SILAS. I'm floating. I'm breathing. We'll get a place, with windows.

They have good years left. With adequate time, we can equalize the imbalance.

MAT. I'm happy for you, man.

SILAS. Mat thank you. Thank you for hiring me, for staking Polly.

MAT. Aw, you redeemed yourself. I just created the conditions. Goes to show anything's possible.

SILAS. Sunlight shines on all.

MAT. What's next?

POLLY. Huh?

MAT. What does the hacker hero do next?

POLLY. It's more about the professor.

MAT. Boring!

POLLY. But...the hacker hero goes to Florida.

MAT. Great great.

POLLY. He adopts his sister.

MAT. Love.

LIN. But she turns against him.

SILAS. *(Positive.)* Oh shit.

LIN. She learns about God Mode and she splits.

MAT. What are the consequences?

LIN. We don't know.

MAT. **Get real about what is at stake.** Don't be afraid to show the pain of rupture.

POLLY. We won't.

MAT. We don't want you to separate, even in the bathroom.

Our highest goals are:

MAT & SILAS. Connect Everyone, Understand the World, and Build the Knowledge Economy.

POLLY. *(To* **LIN**.*)* Allllll the times I was the dumbass. Allllll Polly's bad decisions. You're perfect.

LIN. Me, hah.

POLLY. I'm the fuckup; you steer the course.

LIN. Maladroitly.

POLLY. You could have let me take care of you. You could have made me a person.

LIN. I could have tried.

POLLY. Did some student come with? Did you go by yourself?

LIN. Reyna came.

POLLY. *What.*

LIN. I told you your mom was good to me.

POLLY. *What.*

LIN. It was routine. Still legal. The procedure was five ten minutes –

POLLY. I'M FUCKING HURT!

LIN. There it is.

POLLY. There's what?

LIN. I made a decision about *me*. Furthermore I wrote about it. Publicly. So if you did the work, instead of grabbing shortcuts, you would know me. Care made me a person because at twelve I had the backbone to put your needs before my own.

POLLY. An adult should have helped you. That's not my fault.

LIN. True, but you needed me, and I was there. And I have waited for you to become a sister who might do the same. You were not that person when I terminated. You are not that person now. I long for you to know me. And you come begging to know me. But by what means?

I offered my help. You took my cells.

What will happen to that Tale? Who will feed on my memories? You take what you need when you need it. Now you're hurt? Grow up.

POLLY. I'm grown! You treat me like a baby because I didn't grow into you!

MAT. Gold.

> *(Beat.)*

Silas. You have gone BEYOND with this. It's so ouchy, so spongey. They're pitiful but I vibe them so hard!

SILAS. Same!

MAT. Let's promote you! You're my new right hand.

SILAS. Thanks Mat!

MAT. Help you get a loan to snag that crib for your folks.

SILAS. A loan?

MAT. Well where will they go?

SILAS. They can stay with me.

MAT. In the Sundorm? We don't allow guests. You just need one more bonus.

SILAS. But they're out.

MAT. Keep doing what you do, man. You're so close.

*(To **LIN**.)* And now this department is my think tank. Ethics and the Future of Sunlight.

LIN. You bury information. How can you run a school?

MAT. Not run, own.

Nothing has to change.

LIN. A university is a place to share knowledge.

MAT. Yes, we have a right to know all. I teach my twins, don't let anyone keep you out.

But don't you believe in a world where everyone's voice is heard? Not just the few who jumped the hoops and made the cut?

We'll investigate together.

Let's assert Right to the Dark.

LIN. Fuck off, Mat. I'm meeting with Congress.

        (**JACE** *opens the door.*)

Did you get the exemption?

JACE. They voted against.

LIN. Against Mat?

JACE. Against us.

MAT. The Seeds will Grow! Natural! Unstoppable!

LIN. We regroup.

JACE. The hallway is empty.

LIN. What?

MAT. Your kids are waiting.

LIN. That's tomorrow.

JACE. You messaged moving the day. Or, you didn't?

LIN. My students are –

MAT. In the Dark, now. Awaiting Ethics of Intimacy in the basement of this building, in your unLit lab.

LIN. No one can access the lab.

JACE. Not even me.

LIN. I keep layers of code, for safety.

SILAS. They're in.

MAT. We gotta trust. Isn't that your jam? Just let the hive buzz. Share breath. It's the edge of the Anthropocene. If we don't start breathing together we'll forget how.

LIN. I wrote that two decades ago.

MAT. I read every word.

   (Pleasant.)

Our fragile needy shells. Your precious golden young. Soon we'll nudge up the heat and beam in the Sunlight.

LIN. To a hundred and twelve? Higher?

MAT. Accept my partnership and we'll cool it. But users need a peek at the dark.

POLLY. I'll check on the kids.

LIN. I can go.

POLLY. Let me do this for you.

SILAS. I'll help.

   *(**POLLY** and **SILAS** leave.)*

JACE. Should I go?

LIN. Stay here.

 *(To **MAT**.)* What could you possibly still need?

MAT. I'm not a tech wizard, I'm a heart wizard.

I have so much money. I have more money than the poorest half of the world combined. Money's a game. Money's a joke.

MAT. But romance. Kids. Sisters. These vibe on the same scale. Love makes us equal.

Look at Silas, so devoted to those helpless, broke parents.

LIN. You didn't even know his name.

MAT. Ya caught me.

> *(Pfff sound.)*

I mean, I get what I need to know.

LIN. Why force him into a loan? Why the trick agreements? Keep agreements or you'll never have trust. Without trust you can't be close.

MAT. *(Sincere.)* Really?

LIN. Really.

MAT. Did you report me back then?

LIN. If you had returned you would have been my problem.

MAT. I did return. I am your problem.

LIN. Release my students. Release Polly completely.

MAT. And you offer?

LIN. There might be a way to build something InLight. If you share too.

MAT. How?

LIN. Show all data collected and where it is sold. Show your twins. Show the racial skew of the Underforce camps. Show how hard it is to get out. Show the rest of the planet. Transparent both ways.

MAT. That breaks the magic.

LIN. I'm a professor, you're a mogul, we don't believe in magic.

MAT. I think people are magic. The way we just...sit. And smell different? And our hearts start to beat together.

LIN. Just being with others, in one room, builds empathy. When we lost that, what did we lose? In our return, what can we do?

MAT. We can bring people together.

LIN. I never intended my work to be elite. But conditions have been available only to a few.

MAT. Could I help you with scale?

LIN. What if you fund the gatherings? What if everyone could be included in a Just Us dinner?

MAT. What if everyone could feel how your course felt? When you welcomed me, before I messed up.

LIN. What if you could return to the room?

MAT. I forgot how to be a person.

LIN. I invite you.

    (**LIN** *nods to* **JACE**. **JACE** *turns to us.*)

JACE. *(To us.)* I invite you.

    (**JACE** *walks through the "fourth wall," out of the office, singing to us.*)

IF I COULD OPEN YOUR MOUTH
IF I COULD OPEN YOUR MOUTH
I WOULD REACH
I WOULD REACH
PLACE A BERRY ON YOUR TONGUE
IF YOU COULD OPEN MY MOUTH
IF YOU COULD TOUCH IN MY MOUTH
I WOULD GRANT
YOU THE SAME

    (*This is a different kind of time. We are still seeing a play, but we are aware of the other people in the room.* **JACE** *plays an instrument, talks to us.*)

JACE.   Hey.

I was alone a lot.

I changed a lot.

We share that. We shared not sharing.

It's very awkward to participate.

I'm not going to make you participate.

Except that you are participating. By sharing this room. By being near folks you don't know.

Who's here?

I'm going to try something. We're going to make it very dark.

I'm going to say a first name. If you hear your name, maybe you would be willing to say your name back.

Like, I might hear "Jace"

And I would say "Jace."

If I mispronounce your name, please say it back correctly.

If you just can't do this, or you are not willing to do this, that's perfect.

We'll leave the space for your name, and for you.

> *(It gets totally dark. **JACE** says the name of someone who is actually in the audience. Maybe that person says their name back. **JACE** repeats this about five times, naming real people and waiting for the response.)*

This gathering would not be the same without you.

Do you know that?

Do you really really know that nothing would be the same, without you?

*(**JACE**'s instrument resumes. The lights gently return.)*

I am so glad you made it.

*(**JACE**'s instrument expresses tension, ticking clock.)*

I'm glad I made it.

I wasn't sure, some days.

Some days I am still not sure.

But I know. I have learned. Empirically. In the dark. That nothing would be the same, without me.

*(If health practices allow, **JACE** distributes berries to the audience.)*

It is our right. It is our strength. To know who we are when no one is watching.

To reach for each other.

*(**JACE** leads in all eating a berry together. This is the feeling of a Just Us dinner. If berries happen, cut words in [brackets]. If no berries, keep the words.)*

[Don't worry, not literally. I won't increase your risk.]

[It's scary.]

[It is a scary time.]

You're perfect. You participated perfectly. We, specifically each of us and also all of us, we are here.

*(Lights return to normal. **MAT** and **LIN** onstage, eating berries. **MAT** seems changed.)*

MAT. Like that. More of that.

LIN. Did something happen here we should fight to protect?

MAT. Professor Lin and Sunlight. You and me: the Ethics of Intimacy, everywhere!

LIN. Let's sharpen the part about ethics.

MAT. Sure! Let's! We're partners now! No more loneliness! The future is Lit!

LIN. Turn down the heat on my students.

MAT. Done.

LIN. Restore my sister.

MAT. Of course.

LIN. Begin work. Real work.

MAT. I am ready to work.

LIN. The first step is consent.

MAT. Consent.

LIN. Other people are people. You don't have to invade. We will let you in. It's not too late.

>　　　*(**SILAS** arrives.)*

SILAS. I went down to garden level to let them know the deal.

It's nice and there are windows even, with lead I think?

Frames that look hammered out by hand.

I found the right room.

I opened the door where we'd locked in the kids.

Not kids, emerging adults.

It is an age and a stage.

I should be chilling at that age and stage but I emerged young.

MAT. Should I check it out?

SILAS. No.

I announced myself, said, "This is Silas with Sunlight."

There was a sound like giggles.

It was dark in there. Truly dark.

Growing up like I did you're InLight constantly.

Everything monitored, everything bright.

So I was scared, but I felt the appeal, like: who *am* I when no one's watching?

I suddenly wanted to rest.

LIN. Where's Polly?

SILAS. "This is Silas with Sunlight."

The students were giggling.

They'd swallowed something. A dose of some kind.

They called it, "Lin's secret weapon."

LIN. *(To* **MAT**.*)* You broke the codes that protect the stash.

MAT. I'll stop that behavior.

SILAS. They offered me one. I said yes.

LIN. One should be okay.

SILAS. We are all such cuddle puppies.

MAT. You're on the clock. I'm disappointed.

SILAS. You gave me everything, Mat.

But. That was some antebellum bullshit.

Debtor's badge, Workfarms, Underforce, the whole high tech body harvest.

It's not new.

It's the same boot.

I excel at my job.

SILAS. But freedom should not rest on excellence.

Fifteen years times three lives.

You owe me more than I owe you.

MAT. Let it wear off and we will discuss.

LIN. The dose will wear off. The insight will not.

SILAS. I moved down the hallway, and there was Camille.

(**MAT** *laughs*.)

MAT. Don't fuck with me, man.

SILAS. She let the twins audit Right to the Dark.

They were curious.

It's caught on with kids, like I said.

MAT. *(Tapping his Sunplant.)* Yo Camille, show your smile!

(**POLLY** *enters. Her scar or brand is healed.*)

POLLY. Camille took the boys to the ER.

She said not to come.

MAT. *(Still to Sunplant, in denial of* **POLLY**.*)* Peel back the shield, boys! Game over! Do it! Fucking *now*!

POLLY. They ingested a lot. Many times the grownup dose.

Their hearts stopped.

(*A live vocal drone offstage from* **JACE**.*)*

MAT. Not. my. fam.

POLLY. Camille slung BB and Mazz one on each shoulder, like infants.

I don't know if you heard wailing. It got loud.

I don't know if you heard sirens.

They were delayed due to cuts but Camille had VIP access.

The medics tried to restart their hearts but it's unlikely.

LIN. The stash is not for children. You need a certain body weight. You need a certain size heart.

POLLY. *(To* **MAT**.*)* It was dark and your boys were persuasive.

Here are all Camille's devices. She's done.

Here are the boys' devices.

She doesn't want contact with you.

We had time in the med vac to get clear on that point.

> **(MAT** *bangs his own head.)*

MAT. Camille loves me for me. Camille loves me for me. BB? Mazzie?

> **(MAT** *collapses.)*

Dose me? Overdose me?

> **(MAT** *weeps. Vocal drone stops.)*

LIN. I won't empathize. That was my mistake. You were a sociopath at twenty and I let you go. Your twins were innocent, but so were my students. You threatened to wreck them. I won't feel for you this time.

POLLY. Lin, you're out.

LIN. Me?

POLLY. Camille wants blood.

LIN. Mine?

POLLY. Your methods failed. Your army caused harm.

LIN. Mat violated the safeguards.

POLLY. You put out the call. You said Sunlight is not human.

LIN. The context was –

POLLY. Does this strike you as a time for nuance?

LIN. I'll pack.

POLLY. Leave the books.

LIN. My books?

POLLY. They belong to Sunlight now. I better read them. Silas and I are making a Tale.

The oldest tale in the world.

Light versus Dark.

In the end, equivalent.

LIN. Domination and revolution are not equivalent.

SILAS. You don't know who's good and you don't know who's bad. There are very fine folks on both sides.

MAT. (*A prayer.*) Take me out of God Mode.

LIN. It's done.

> (**LIN** *moves to go.*)

POLLY. You can live with me until you get a new job.

LIN. I have no home?

POLLY. Lean on me a minute. I'm your sister. I'm grown.

My eggs are safe. I paid years in advance.

I'll harvest at the right time and you'll be Boss Auntie. But first, our Tale.

SILAS. Now with the codes cracked, we can access all records. The whole library. Behind the university paywall, history goes back years.

POLLY. Even a decade. We will have so much context now.

SILAS. We will flip this one eighty. We will lay down new norms.

After this loss. We are gonna build from the memories of BB and Mazz. We will bear witness. We will shine truth, for the future.

LIN. And I?

POLLY. You're Professor Lin.

LIN. I was.

POLLY. And I'm gonna know you. I promise.

(**POLLY** *and* **LIN** *reach for each other.*)

LIN. No.

POLLY. No?

LIN. I don't trust you.

POLLY. That's pathology. You're the big sister, you had to be everything for everyone.

LIN. My love for you was bottomless.

POLLY. I know.

(**JACE** *appears in a protective garment, carrying supplies. Perhaps a wound near the neck.*)

LIN. Did you dose?

JACE. I am sober.

We cut out our Sunplants.

It hurt.

We have maps. We have masks. We are ready to try.

We will head for the Outer Plains.

You taught us who we are when no one is watching.

Come claim our Right to the Dark.

(**JACE** *extends a hand.* **LIN** *takes it.*)

*(**LIN** extends a hand, inviting **POLLY**. **POLLY** stays.)*

POLLY. Lin, forgive me.

LIN. No one is disposable.

*(**JACE** and **LIN** go. **POLLY** wraps herself in the Lin garment she wore in the Tale. She is the avatar.)*

(Lights brighten to a cheery new normal.)

SILAS. We're going to get this Tale right.

We will see each other fully. In bright truth. Aboveground.

POLLY. And yet be kind of cozy?

SILAS. It is a New Golden Age.

And I'm pumped!

End of Play

Jace's Song 1

Karen Hartman

Eerie folk vibe

Jace's Song 2

Karen Hartman

Yearning, rhythm can be loose